On Sand Island

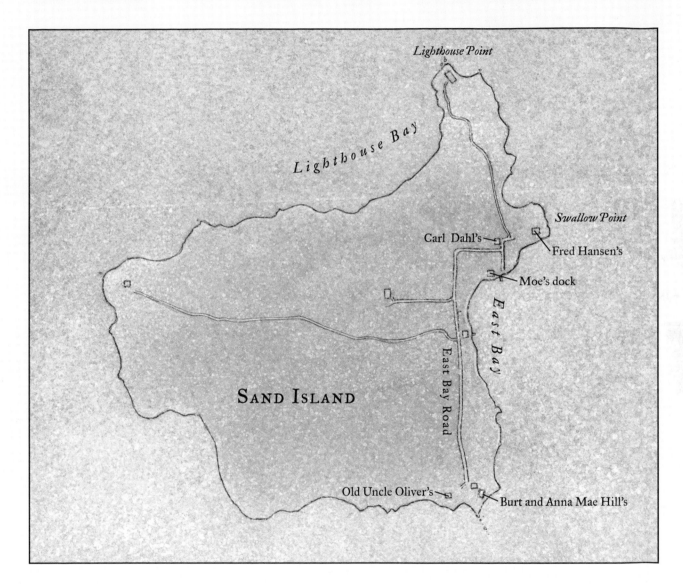

Lighthouse Point

Lighthouse Bay

Swallow Point

Carl Dahl's

Fred Hansen's

Moe's dock

East Bay

East Bay Road

SAND ISLAND

Old Uncle Oliver's

Burt and Anna Mae Hill's

Jacqueline Briggs Martin   *Illustrated by* David Johnson

HOUGHTON MIFFLIN COMPANY
BOSTON 2003

For my family
—J.B.M.

For Wes
—D.J.

www.houghtonmifflinbooks.com

The text of this book is set in HTF Fell Type Roman.
The illustrations are ink and watercolor on paper.
Frontispiece inspired by map in *Diary of a Norwegian Fisherman* [edited by Frederick H. Dahl,
published by Paramount Press, 1989], a journal kept from 1913 to 1938 by Fred Hansen.

Library of Congress Cataloging-in-Publication Data

Martin, Jacqueline Briggs.
On Sand Island / Jacqueline Briggs Martin ; illustrated by David A. Johnson.
p. cm.
Summary: In 1916 on an island in Lake Superior, Carl builds himself
a boat by bartering with the other islanders for parts and labor.
ISBN 0-618-23151-X [hardcover]
[1. Islands—Fiction. 2. Boats and boating—Fiction. 3. Barter—Fiction.
4. Superior, Lake—Fiction.] I. Johnson, David A., ill. II. Title.
PZ7.M363168 On 2003
[Fic]—dc21
2002005090

Printed in Singapore
TWP 10 9 8 7 6 5 4 3 2 1

ACKNOWLEDGMENTS

I want to thank the National Park Service for the Artist-in-Residency grant, which allowed me to spend time on Sand Island. I'm especially grateful to Carl Dahl, Jr., for building a boat with me using Burt Hill's old saw and for sharing many island stories about his father—the Carl in this story—and others. Thanks also to Sharon Dahl for providing a workplace for our boat-building and suitable lumber; to Frederick Dahl for compiling Fred Hansen's diaries into such a wonderful resource; and to Connie Dahl and Bob Dahl for sharing photographs and island memories. Thanks also to Bob and Susan Mackreth of the National Park Service, Dick and LaDonna Palm, and Nancy Peterson for sharing resources, stories, and their love of Sand Island. Such stories and details were lumber, too—lumber that went into this story of life on Sand Island.

N.B. Sand Islanders will tell you "pound" boat is pronounced *pond* boat. —J.B.M

CARL'S POCKETS

WHEN LAKE SUPERIOR WAS THICK WITH FISH
and strung with nets,
and fishermen found their way on the water
by watching the sun,
a Sand Island boy named Carl
put salt in his pocket every morning.
He knew—because Old Uncle Oliver had told him—
if he could throw salt on a live rabbit's tail
he could make a wish,
and the wish would come true.
That was his good-luck pocket.

In his other pocket
he kept the green beach glass
he and his mother had found
four summers ago,
when Carl was only six.
His mother had been gone since last fall,
carried to Bayfield in a coffin
on the roof of a fishing boat.
But Carl had the glass,
rubbed smooth by the lake
and his own hand.
That was his keep-away-bad-luck pocket.

SAND ISLAND LUCK

Bad luck on Sand Island
was a five-day storm,
which meant Carl's father couldn't lift his nets
and pick out the fish caught in their mesh.
Bad luck was a cold, sister-still-sleeping kitchen
when Carl got up in the morning.
Bad luck was getting to Moe's dock too late
to see the *C.W. Turner* drop off the mail.
And bad luck was standing at the edge of the water
when he could be out in a boat.

Good luck on Sand Island was
a big lift of fish in his father's nets.
On those bright days
his father played Norway folk songs
on the harmonica.
His sister put on their mother's best scarf—
the red wool—
and they danced in the kitchen.

Good luck was a piece of Anna Mae Hill's coconut cake—
sweet and crumbly and covered with cream
whipped so thick fishermen said they could stand on it.
Good luck was afternoon-rafting along East Bay.
But the best luck for Carl
would be having his own boat.

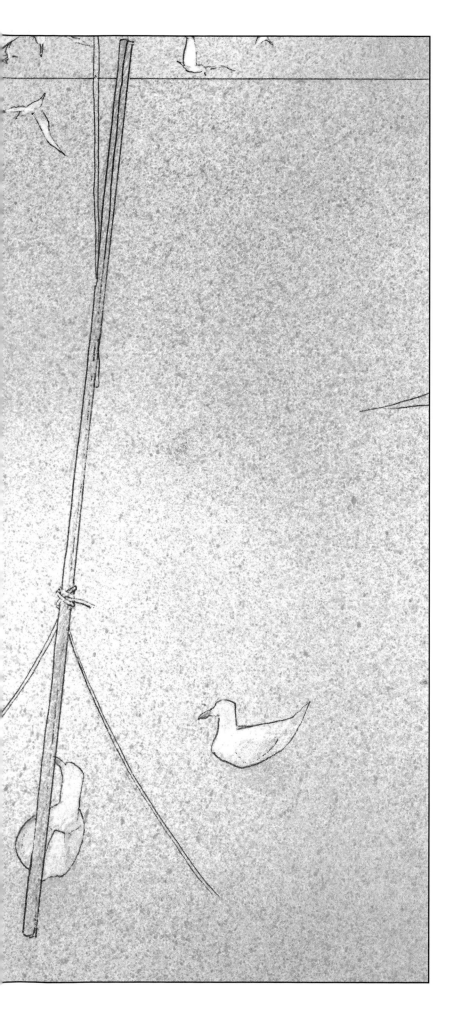

BOATS

CARL WANTED A BOAT OF HIS OWN
more than a new bicycle.
A boat could take him out
away from the too-quiet house,
away from his sister's lumpy, no-salt, no-sugar meals.
A boat could take him out
where the quiet was filled
with water and sky.

Carl dreamed about boats.
He drew the boat he would build:
a little flat-bottomed pound boat,
like the fishermen use
who set poles and nets in the lake
to make fences for fish.
"You're too young to build a boat," his sister said.
"It will sink
before you get past Moe's dock.
And we'll lose you, too."

THE BEGINNING

THEN CAME THE DAY
Carl found the boards
floated in off the lake—
long, wide boards
to cut and hammer into a boat.

Hummingbirds ate from jewelweed flowers,
while Carl tugged those boards
up from the beach
to the grass beside his father's fish shed.
That was the end of the hard work,
he told himself.
Sawing would be easy.

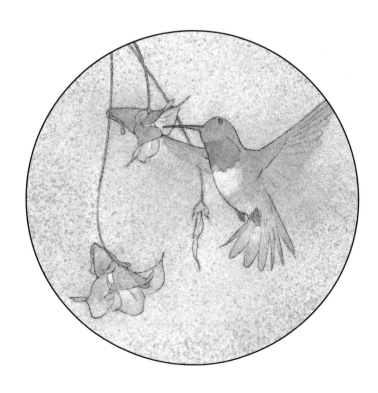

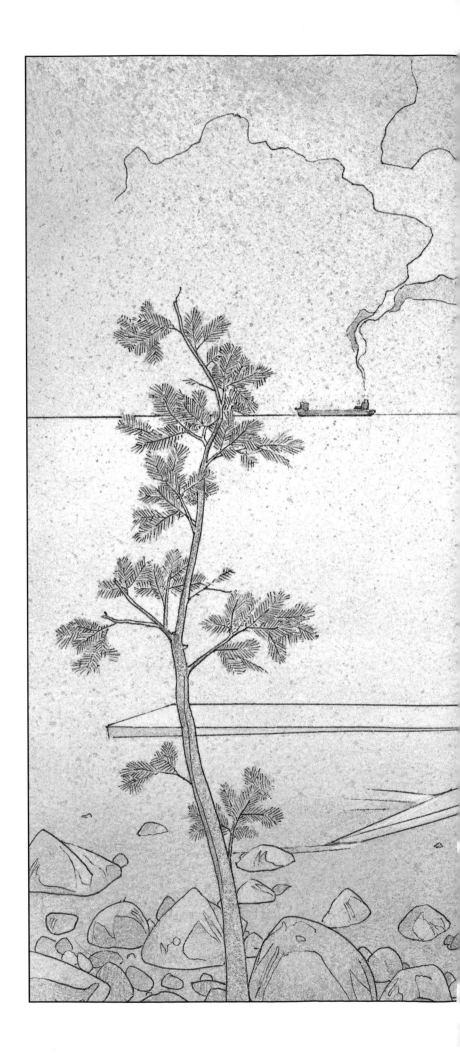

WORK FOR WORK

THE NEXT MORNING
Carl's father went out on the water
to drop nets in the place of
"fire in the branches," the place
where he could see the sun through the trees
at Lighthouse Point.
Carl looked at his boards
and imagined himself in his new boat,
rowing so close to ducks
he could count their feathers.

But the saw stuck in the wood
or took quick jumps
and scratched his hands.
Carl couldn't make it cut.
His sister was busy washing clothes.
His father would be out until supper.

Perhaps their neighbor Torvald,
a little man who whistled all day
and built rocking chairs from fish barrels,
would trade work for work.

Torvald said,
"Sure, I'll cut your wood,
if you'll pick my strawberries.
The *C. W. Turner* comes tomorrow
and will take them to sell in Bayfield."

Carl picked strawberries all afternoon.
He picked until he thought
he'd always walk a little bit stooped,
like Old Uncle Oliver.
Torvald sawed the wood
and stacked it in a pile.

That night Carl said,
"That's the end of the hard work.
Nailing will be easy."

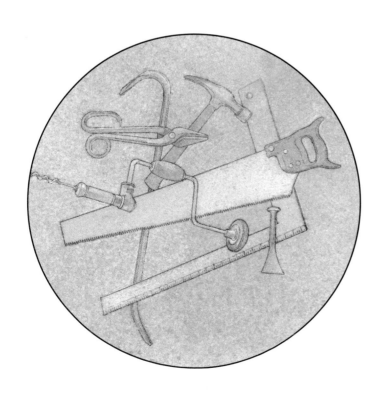

BURT HILL

THE NEXT MORNING
Carl looked at the pile of boards
and imagined he was boating
in the caves by Swallow Point,
looking for pictures drawn on the rocks
by the First People who lived on Sand Island.

But he was stopped
when he found no nails in the fish shed.
He didn't want to pick strawberries again.
Then Carl thought of Burt Hill.

Burt Hill was a saver. His shop
was filled with scraps of metal, pieces of wood,
and cans of used nails, hinges, bolts, and screws.
The shop's best place was the wall
where Burt wrote down
what he saved for memory:

> *Summer* 1910. Moved to Sand Island. Tore down the old fish
> shed. Used the lumber on the house.
>
> *November* 1911. Boat broke down twice on lake. Got home—
> but covered in ice, stem to stern.
>
> *June* 1913. Capt. Lee towed raft of logs through my pound nets
> and ruined them for the season.
>
> *May* 28, 1914. Our Marguerite graduated from Bayfield High
> School. We went to watch. M. came home with us.
>
> *November* 1915. Anna Mae and M. cooked like two steam
> engines for large crew of herring fishermen.

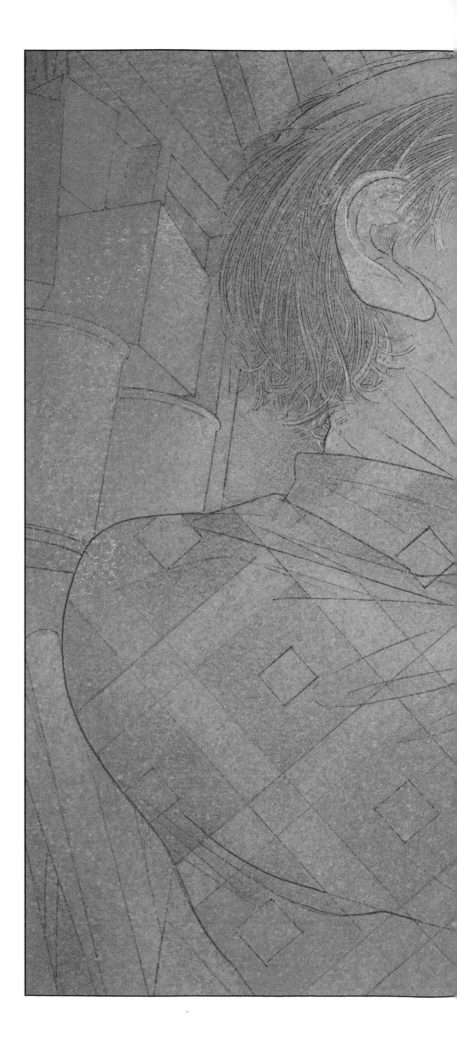

Burt Hill smelled of pipe smoke
and the peppermints
he carried in a small paper bag.
He always let Carl pick candy out of the bag.

"Sure, I've got nails," Burt said.
"Help me move these rocks under my dock
so it won't float away in high water.
Anna Mae won't let you work without lunch.
After we eat we'll go and look at your boat."

They loaded rocks as big as pumpkins
onto the stone drag,
hauled them along the beach,
and dropped them inside the crib,
which would hold them under the dock.

Carl's arms were sore that night.
But he looked at his boat—nailed tight,
and snug with caulking cotton—and said,
"That's the last of the hard work.
Painting will be easy."

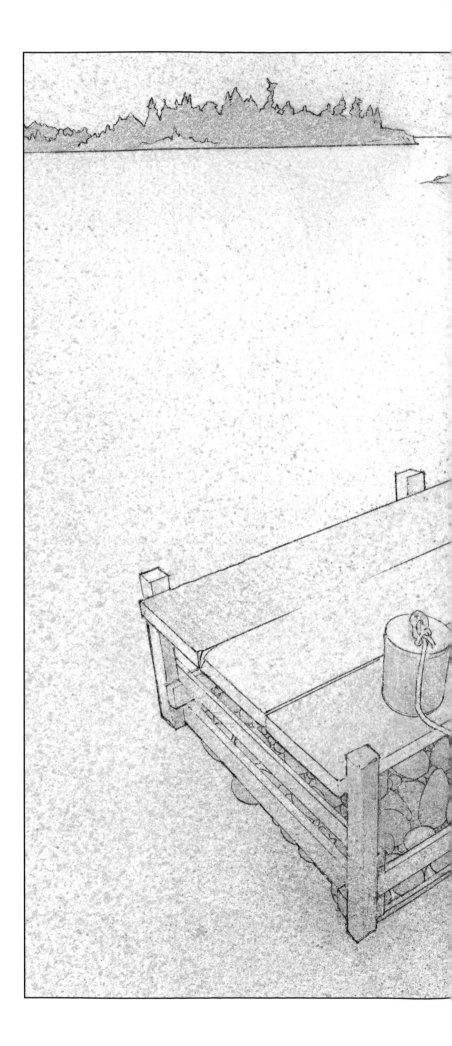

KEEPING OUT THE WATER

THE NEXT MORNING
Carl sat in his boat
and saw himself out in Lighthouse Bay,
catching fish for Sunday dinner.
But he needed paint to seal the joints
or his boat would sink
before he got to Lighthouse Bay.
He had no paint.

Perhaps Fred Hansen could help.
The Hansens were neighbors,
and island neighbors are closer than cousins.
Carl found the fisherman busy with nets.
"I'll fix nets," the boy said, "in trade for paint."
So they sewed cedar floats—corks—
to a line at the top of the nets
and pounded lead weights to a line at the bottom.
The nets, made of string
fine enough for a baby's hat,
would stand straight in the water—
invisible snags for whitefish and trout.

By the time they finished, Carl thought
he would see fishnets
whenever he closed his eyes.

But just before supper,
he looked at his boat,
sealed and shiny with paint,
and said,
"That's the end of the hard work."

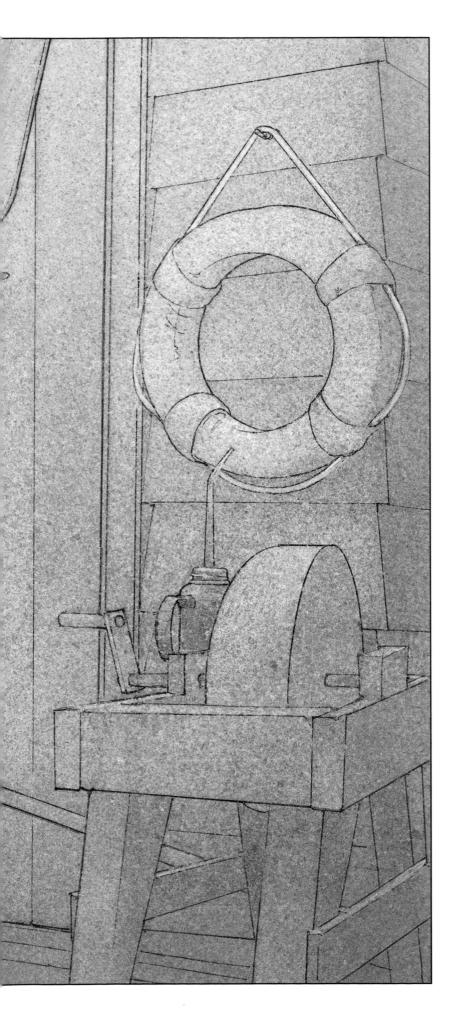

THE OLD OARS

THE NEXT MORNING
spiders made webs on thimbleberry leaves.
Carl's sister churned cream into butter.
Carl's father said,
"That's a right boat you've built.
But you'll need some oars."
He went to a back corner of the fish shed
and found two oars.
"These are old—from Norway.
You can clean them up
while your paint dries and cures."

Carl sanded off the dirt and bad wood.
He thought he could have sandpapered the entire fish shed
in the time it took him to fix up those splintery oars.
As the sun was setting
off Lighthouse Point,
Carl said, "That's the last of the hard work."

And he was right.

Boat Celebration

In the morning
Carl walked to the water and looked at his boat.
His sister had come before him
and set up their mother's red scarf for a flag.

While island rabbits ate grass under bushes
Carl took the boat out on the water.
He rowed close enough to ducks in East Bay
to count their feathers.
He rowed next to the caves
and looked for secret pictures
from the First People.
He caught three fish
as long as his arm.

His father said they should celebrate
the newest boat on the island.
His sister made Carl's favorite stew
of fish and butter and milk.
She asked Carl to add salt from his good-luck pocket.

Burt and Anna Mae Hill
came with coconut cream cake.
Fred Hansen and his family
came with bustle and warm bread.
Old Uncle Oliver came with a fiddle.
Neighbor Torvald came with strawberry jam.

They ate together,
danced, and sang,
and everyone said Carl would make a fine boatman.

Then they went home to sleep
and wait for the sun to rise
on another day on Sand Island.

Author's Note

A BOY NAMED CARL—Carl Dahl—really did live on Sand Island in the early 1900s. And he did grow up to be a fisherman. After his father was lost on the lake in April 1928, Carl returned from the U.S. Navy to Sand Island, raised a family, and fished Lake Superior, setting his nets in the place where he could see fire in the branches.

But in the 1940s sea lampreys came into Lake Superior, fastened their round, rough mouths on the lake's whitefish and trout, and killed them without nets or hooks. They killed so many fish that a fisherman could no longer make a good living. In 1952, Carl moved to Sault Ste. Marie and operated tugboats, but he returned to Sand Island every summer for the rest of his life. The National Park Service ranger's cabin on the island sits where Carl Dahl and his family lived.

People still say Carl Dahl was one of the finest men and one of the best boatmen ever to live on Sand Island.

Sand Island

Bayfield

Lake Superior

Sault Ste. Marie